SAFE HAVEN

A REACHER SERIES SHORT STORY

L E FITZPATRICK

Read more about L E Fitzpatrick

https://www.facebook.com/lefitzpatrickbooks

THE REACHER SERIES

The Running Game
Border Lines
Every Storm Breaks
Family
The Lost Shepherd

I have to make it quick. The army is moving in, so we're moving out. Don't worry. They've found a place for me in Safe Haven. At a hospital. After all this time we can finally be together again. I miss you, but we'll be together soon. I might even be in S'aven by the time you get this letter. Come find me.

   Rachel

1

The world was white. So white the night time shadows couldn't penetrate the layers of snow suffocating the forest. Each breath Isobel managed to push out crystallised, sparkling under the moonlight. The snow swallowed her legs in hungry gulps. Her hands and feet were numb, but her thighs burned furiously with each step.

It was late and she was so very tired. The previous night was spent in the back of their family Land Rover, fighting for space on the backseat with her little sister while Dad kept watch. It had been a cold, broken night, but Isobel would give anything to be back there. Anything not to be walking through Red Forest in the middle of December.

She sniffed and looked behind her. Rachel was six, only three years younger but at that moment it felt like a lifetime between them. Rachel didn't understand why they were in the middle of the wilderness. She had no idea why they had to leave Mum. She had slept through their uncle screaming the soldiers were coming. She had no idea of the danger they were in. Isobel stared at her sister as she struggled in the snow, envying every tiny, oblivious step she took.

Rachel fell and started to cry. She was sobbing for Mum. Isobel knew they would never see their mother again. She took a strong, heavy breath, close to tears herself. She wanted to move to help her sister, but her legs refused to go back, not after the effort made in going forwards.

Instead she called out. "Dad!"

He was ahead of them, scoping out the safety of the path. When he saw Rachel he hurried back, covering the ground in five easy strides. He lifted Rachel in his large arms and brushed the snow from her hair.

Then the gunfire started.

"Run!" Dad screamed.

Light sparked through the trees, as though the night sky had sunk to the earth. Isobel was transfixed.

"Izzy!"

Men shaped shadows followed the light. They were coming. Her feet leapt into her father's footsteps. With Rachel in his arms, he weaved through the trees. The foliage became denser, the snow thinner. Her feet struck firming soil, frozen dirt, icy puddles. The ground started to dip. She jumped and her father caught her. He pulled her close and they huddled together in a burrow off the path.

"We need to work together." He whispered so softly Isobel thought she was imagining him. "We're not here," he told them. "Say it with me. We're not here."

Isobel closed her eyes, sinking into her father's waxed coat. She reached for her sister's hand and concentrated. "We're not here," she repeated. "We're not here." Over and over she focussed on the words, hearing the echo in the deep voice of her father and the squeak of her sister.

Time started to twist, the cold subsided and she felt herself floating. The explosions, the shouting, the danger, all started to melt away. There was an energy engulfing her. But it wasn't hers, it didn't even belong to her father. The dominant voice inside her head became her sister's, small and yet commanding. She focused on it and felt herself merge into nothing.

How long had they stayed like that? Isobel had no idea. When her father broke free of their spell the militia had gone. The surrounding trees were torn apart with gunshot. Pieces of bark and bullet shells were scattered the ground around them. It had been ferocious what-ever had come their way.

"Daddy?" Rachel asked. "What's going on?"

Isobel waited. She'd asked the question herself the night before, but she was sure Dad wouldn't repeat himself. How could he tell a six year old the truth? That they were caught in the middle of a civil war, insurgents and militia intent on claiming land that never belonged to them. How could he explain to her that these men didn't care who got caught in the crossfire? That this wasn't a fight for free-dom, or liberty, or any sense of lost righteousness? That this was about control and power? How could he tell his youngest daughter that she had never been in more danger, because if they found out what she was, what all three of them were, both sides would lock them away?

"We're playing a game," he said, stroking his younger daughter's hair. "The running game remember. We have to run and hide, concentrate on not getting caught. Wherever we go, whatever we do we keep moving, counting the exits, planning our escape so nobody can ever find us."

"It sounds like a stupid game," Rachel said.

Dad laughed. "It does, but you get a prize if you play it well."

"What prize?"

"You get to grow up. You have to keep running, baby. Always be ready to run because they'll always be coming for you. Whatever happens, they'll always be coming for you." He held Rachel close, protecting her from the next confession. "They'll never stop," he said. "Right now, we need to rest. The secret to winning the game is knowing when to run and when to wait. You're both tired. You've done so well today. Sleep now and we'll try to get out of the forest in a few hours."

Rachel was asleep in moments. Isobel had a suspicion Dad had used his powers. She snored quietly, looking almost peaceful.

"There's a lot of ground to cover," he said to Isobel. "We're going to make our way south, to Safe Haven. There's a man there. A priest called Father Darcy. He's an old friend. We can trust him. He'll help hide us until all this is over."

Isobel nodded. These were instructions, not reassurances. She rolled the name in her head; Father Darcy. She had to remember it.

"Your sister, her powers..." He shook his head and sighed. "If they find her it will be bad for all Reachers." He turned to her, his eyes warming. "If they find either of you, it will be bad, honey. You need to be strong. You need to look after your sister. I wouldn't trust her to anyone else." He pushed the hair from her face. "My beautiful girl, look at you, you're so grown up already. "

She felt a lump swell in her throat.

"Whatever happens, you look after your sister. Can you do that, Izzy?"

Her father was a good man, she would have done anything to make him happy. She stared into his dark eyes and they betrayed everything that was about to come—his death, their journey, her future.

"Can you?"

Would he have asked if he had known what it would mean—what she would do to keep her sister safe?

"Isobel?"

2

"Isobel?"

She turned and looked at the man in the doorway, tapping his foot. Frank Morris was in his forties, but time had not been kind. His face was imprinted with aggressive creases. His body tightly coiled, ready to spring apart at any moment. Sensible people were scared of Frank, and the fuzzy scarf Isobel had bought him for Christmas did nothing to soften his appeal. She loved him, after a decade of being in his care he had naturally assumed the role of her father. But love and loathing were not mutually exclusive. Isobel was old enough now to understand that the things he had asked of her, asked when she was just a child, were not the requests of a good man. And yet she still loved him in a way.

He stared at her. Expectant. Impatient.

"Sorry, did you say something?"

"My phone, have you seen it?"

She glanced around his office. It was nowhere obvious. "Maybe you left it at home."

He grumbled and checked his watch. "We're late. We're not going to make the reservation at this rate." Frank stormed from the office to tear apart the rest of the club.

Frank had been her surrogate father for ten years. Ten years today since he had brought her home, into a house that was as big as a palace, filled with presents and food and festive cheer. Where had all that gone? She shook her head, it was all still there, but it was like the heavy makeup on her thinning face, hiding an awful truth—total emptiness.

"Izzy!" he bellowed from the other room. "We're late, move it."

She hurried out of the office, crossing the empty dancefloor. When she reached the door, Frank was already waiting for her, an umbrella outstretched to protect them both from the downpour. She stayed close as they walked to the car, keeping a watchful eye on the street.

Today Frank was driving. Their last driver had been—Isobel looked at the driver's seat—*untrustworthy*. That was the word she had whispered in Frank's ear. He didn't like Frank, he thought Frank was an asshole, and so he was dealt with. After that Frank couldn't find anyone to drive for them so he got his man Donnie to do it. But it was Donnie's day off, so he did it himself.

She strapped herself into the passenger seat and watched Frank as he pulled away. He used to be a good looking man but time had taken its toll. The days of the all powerful Frank Morris were slipping away. As she sat there, ten years to the day they had met, she wondered if she was the reason it had all gone wrong for him.

"You're quiet," he said.

"I'm just thinking," she said.

"Thinking about what?"

"When we met. What things were like back then."

"Back before we had everyone running scared." He thought fear was power. He was wrong.

Isobel sighed. "I remember when you brought me home. I was so scared. You had this big house, that huge bedroom, all those presents. I couldn't believe it, I'd never seen so many fancy boxes. And you said they were all for me."

"I spoilt you."

"Yes." If she had known what awaited her in the years to come, would she have unwrapped those gifts so eagerly? "Yes, you did."

3

"Girls. Girls wake up. We have to go."

Dad pulled Rachel up and reached for Isobel. The light was strange. Isobel couldn't tell if the day was starting or ending. It shimmered unnaturally through the trees, illuminating the snow in shades of yellow and orange. She stood up in a daze, watching the leaves quiver and shudder. Wisps of bark danced in the air. She frowned as a wooden shard struck her face.

The treeline mutated. There were men everywhere. Her hand was pulled. She started to run. The snow worked against them, snatching at Rachel's legs and Isobel's ankles. Isobel felt something rush by her ear. Something else by her neck. Bullets shredded the air. She kept pace with Dad, twisting her body as she leapt over a fallen tree.

Her lungs were burning. Her cheeks freezing. And all she could do was move. Move faster. Push harder. Don't stop. *Run, run, as fast as you can.* Her ankle twisted. She fought through the pain.

"Daddy!"

Rachel's voice tore through the forest, battering the bullets into silence. Isobel turned. Her father was already running back. Rachel was on her knees. He snatched her from the floor and turned to run. *One step. Two step.* The first bullet hit him in the shoulder. *Three step. Four step*. Isobel started running towards him. *Five step*. His neck sprayed with blood. Isobel screamed. Her fingertips grazed his head as he fell forward, Rachel still in his arms.

His fingers twitched against the snow. White turning red. Isobel stopped screaming. He was gone. She'd lost him. She saw movement under his body. *Rachel*. On her hands and knees she rolled her father's corpse over and pulled her sister free. Rachel was drenched in her father's blood. Her eyes fixed in fear. She tried to wipe her face clean, checking for holes in her little body. Nothing.

Isobel took her hands. *Look after your sister*. The bullets rained harder. Isobel pulled Rachel forward. It was just them now.

4

"Have a look in the glove box, would you?" Frank said, still checking his pockets as he drove.

Isobel opened the glove box and pulled out an assortment of maps and weapons. "No phone," she said. "Why do you want it so badly?"

She was probably the only person in the world who could challenge Frank Morris and walk away from the conversation.

"I need to speak to Donnie."

"You gave him the day off"

"Yeah, but I wanted him to drive us, so we could celebrate properly."

"He's not your driver. And he doesn't get a lot of time to himself, leave him be."

Frank raised his greying eyebrow. "You bossing me around now?" He meant it playfully, but habit applied a threatening tone to his voice.

Isobel knew better and ignored him. She put the things back away in the glove box and returned to looking out of the window. It was raining in S'aven, pouring in thick blankets over the city. The power was out, short fused last month by the lights people still insisted on having this time of year. For one night in December the city was lit up like a warzone and then bang! The world was plunged into darkness and Isobel was left with nothing but the empty road.

5

The road into the mountain was torn up. Large chunks had been blasted apart by mortar and rockets and God only knows what else those soldiers used to destroy each other. It was a challenge to try and navigate through it as dusk fell, leaving them with only a thin strip of moonlight seeping through the trees. They had to push on as fast as their aching legs would permit. Isobel held her sister's hand, guiding her around the rubble and icy patches as best she could. Rachel's lips were blue and her eyes glassy, both of which were enough to distract Isobel from the frozen blood on her sister's clothes.

"There's a man in Safe Haven who's going to help us," she told Rachel, trying to keep her voice steady. "Dad told me we have to go there. We'll get to Safe Haven and we'll be okay."

Safe Haven was just outside the capital in the south of England. They were more than 250 miles north. Isobel had no idea how long it would take, but they would make it, she had promised Dad she would take care of Rachel.

Their steps slowed but persisted down the road. Then Rachel stopped. She pulled on Isobel's hand as headlights struck both girls. *Don't speak to strangers.* She'd heard it so many times and her heart lurched. But Rachel stayed firm. Another night in the cold and they would both be dead. Whoever, whatever was in that car was their only chance.

The vehicle came to an abrupt halt. Isobel stared into the headlights. Was this what her father saw in his final moments; a glowing light promising sanctuary without substance? The driver's door opened and a large figure peered out of the vehicle, looking as shaken as Isobel felt.

"You girls okay?" the driver said.

Rachel looked to her sister and gave her an encouraging nod.

"Are you hurt?"

"No, sir," Isobel said. "Our dad..." Her voice started to croak. She gestured to the trees, hoping he would understand.

"Do you live around here?" the man said, coming closer to them. Isobel sensed his nervousness, he was expecting an ambush.

"We lived near here, before the soldiers came."

The man's white beard hid most of his red face. His eyes were hard and sharp. He wore a thick jacket, well-worn and patched up in places, over several layers of woollen jumpers, making him appear bigger than he really was. Isobel thought she recognised him. Their community was spread out over acres and acres, but with such a limited population their paths crossed often. She caught the man giving her a similar look, as though he were trying to place the two girls from a Christmas market, or bonfire night before the fighting broke out.

"There are soldiers in the forest. They killed our father."

The man scowled at the trees, reluctant to help. Isobel reached for his hand, allowing her fingers to brush the exposed skin of his wrist.

"Aye, okay. You'd best come with me. I'll take you girls home."

"No, please sir. We need to go to Safe Haven."

He paused, transfixed. "That's a long way away."

Rachel grabbed his other hand. "Please take us to Safe Haven," she pleaded.

Whatever thoughts he had, wherever he was going, no longer mattered. The girls controlled him. Isobel guided him to the car, she took the passenger seat. Rachel crawled in the back and wrapped herself in the extra coat he kept there.

"I'm hungry," Rachel said.

"There's some protein cans on the floor there." The man started the engine. "You girls get settled in, I'll get you to S'aven don't you worry."

6

She was waiting for Frank to bring up Donnie again. He didn't. It meant he either didn't know, or he did and he was playing a game with her. He liked to do that, twist things to trap people. Donnie was Frank's right hand. He was loyal. More loyal than Frank realised or appreciated. The Scotsman was one of the few people who would willingly give his life for the gangster.

Their affair—was it even an affair? —was still blossoming. To the outside, Donnie was a deranged psychopath and Frank's rabid hell hound. For Isobel, he was a loyal guard dog and friend. He was close to Isobel in years and being one of the few people Frank truly trusted, he was permitted a friendship with her. To this day he hadn't laid a finger in lust or anger on Isobel, she suspected he never would. But he did listen to her, he did sympathise with her, he did support her.

She wasn't sure what Frank would do when he found out—which he would, he always did. He liked Isobel for himself, keeping her like an antique doll, never to be played with. He didn't care that she was lonely. She belonged to him and he didn't like to share. For just the potential of a relationship, Donnie would likely be euthanized.

7

His name was Bill. He never married, never had children. He used to have a dog and he loved that dog so much. He told the girls about it as he drove and for a little while all Isobel could think about was Bill and his dog, walking through the tranquil forest, hunting rabbits and never worrying about anything more than the car battery going flat. It was a good life and he had been happy. Isobel couldn't imagine ever being happy again.

Bill drove the back roads to Safe Haven as though he instinctively knew to keep the girls hidden from the motorway patrols. Isobel watched with wonder as the familiar trees and hills fell away and the landscape flattened into a barren nothingness. The barest signs of community clustered in groups on the edges of large roads. The people she saw were dishevelled loners. Winter had claimed Britain and civilisation was in hibernation.

Then they began approaching Safe Haven and the world seemed to exhale into life. The roads grew busier, the streets started to move with people. An empty horizon suddenly exploded in concrete and machinery. Isobel leaned forward, staring at an urban landscape. She felt like an alien, landing in civilisation for the first time.

A sign reached out from the tarmac: Welcome to Safe Haven.

Isobel felt herself sigh in relief. They had made it. She noticed the atmosphere in the car shift. Bill was starting to get anxious and confused. His mission was over and, without the girls' instructions, he was starting to regain his senses. Isobel reached out and put her hand on his as it clasped the steering wheel.

"You can let us out here," she said.

He frowned. "Leave you here? By yourselves?"

"You can let us out and then go somewhere safe," Isobel told him.

He pulled up the car in a daze. "You girls sure you're going to be okay out here on your own?"

Rachel leaned forward and gave him a kiss on his cheek. "Thank you Bill," she said. "I hope you get another dog."

Bill drove off as soon as they got out of the car. Neither girl stopped to wave him off. The bustle of the streets immediately overwhelmed them. Rachel's hand found Isobel's and the pair froze.

"Where are we going?" Rachel whispered.

Isobel straightened her back. "I told you before. We're going to find the man Dad told us about. Darcy. That's where we're going. And everything is going to be okay."

She didn't know it at the time but the church was hidden from the outside world and yet obvious to a Reacher. She could feel a calling as soon as they were in the city and, without talking, both girls moved closer towards the secret church, currently hidden in a small terraced house a few streets from the market. They reached it before their first night in Safe Haven, before the rain and frost had any chance to claim them.

Isobel knocked on a painted green door with a handmade holly wreath adorning it. She was certain they were in the right place. An old man opened the door. He was wearing his collar in defiance of the persecution of religion in the city. A thinning crop of greying curls drew Isobel's eye. Darcy was stocky, managing to look ancient and youthful at the same time. His dark eyes stared down at the girls in unrestrained kindness.

"Come in, girls, come in," he said, soothing them with his rich Caribbean accent. "You're safe now."

There wasn't a lot to his church. The front room was set out to receive devotees, with chairs and a crude altar. The advent took pride of place in the centre of the table, two candles lit at Christ's feet. Darcy led them past that room and through to the kitchen. He gestured that the girls sit at the table and poured them both a glass of mulled spices from a pan cooking on the gas stove. Isobel sipped at hers, ignoring the funny taste. Rachel pushed hers aside and crinkled her nose.

"Now, let me see if I can get this right." He wagged a finger at Isobel. "You must be Isobel and this must be Rachel."

"How do you know our names?" Isobel asked.

"Your dad told me all about you." Darcy didn't ask about their father—the stains on Rachel's dress said enough.

"Are you girls hungry?"

They both nodded.

"Well then, I better start cooking. Isobel, if you take your sister upstairs there's some hot water in the bath and some clothes in the room next door. You get yourselves cleaned up. Help yourselves to anything you like and we'll have ourselves a nice dinner when you're ready." Darcy turned to his kitchen, as if having two refugees showing up at his door was normal.

"How did you know we were coming?" Rachel asked.

Darcy looked back at them. "The man upstairs told me." He gave Rachel a wink and went back to cooking.

Rachel tugged on Isobel's hand. "Who's upstairs?"

8

Isobel smiled to herself as Frank pulled the car around the back of a butcher's shop.

"What's so funny?" He always got suspicious when he thought he was missing a joke.

"Just thinking about when I first met Darcy, back when he had hair."

Finally, Frank cracked a smile. "Jesus, he did, didn't he? I had forgotten about that."

The butcher's storeroom was the latest home for the Church of Reachers. Since she'd known Darcy, he'd had five places in S'aven and spent two years roaming Britain and going wherever God led him. It didn't matter where the church ended up, she always got that feeling of coming home whenever she was with Darcy.

He was waiting for them inside, as much at home surrounded by hanging carcasses as he was sitting at a kitchen table. He shook Frank's hand first, but his attention, as always, would soon fix on Isobel.

"How's it going, Darcy?" Frank asked, shaking the old priest's hand with enthusiasm.

"Same old, same old. Worthy cause and an uphill struggle. I've got some paperwork for you. Come see where your money is being spent."

Frank was the biggest donator to the secret church. He put everything he could into Darcy's hands to help the priest in his quest to save Reachers like Isobel and her sister. For all the awful things Frank had done—continued to do—this was his redemption. His money had saved countless Reachers, paying for their travel, documents, food, clothing. It was Frank's money that paid for Rachel's safety.

Isobel remembered that fact every time she returned to Darcy. Sometimes she thought that was why Frank brought her here; so she would feel grateful for what he had done and the sacrifices she had made herself wouldn't seem so bad. It worked usually, but today her past was weighing heavily.

She embraced Darcy. As usual she found the altar and spent a few moments alone with Christ. *Forgive me for what I have done, for what I will do.* She had never prayed for her sister, never in all these years. She didn't have to, she had control of Rachel's future. She did what Frank wanted and he paid to keep Rachel safe in the convent. At least that was how it had been. She stared at the crude carving of Christ on the wall. *Please keep my sister safe. Please keep her out of S'aven.*

A hand touched her shoulder. She turned around, surprised to see Darcy had occupied Frank so easily. He always tried to distract Frank with some article or news story about Reachers so he could have a few moments alone with Isobel. These moments were a highlight for her, and today they were a necessity.

"The letter you gave me from Rachel. Do you know what was in it?"

Darcy gave a regretful nod. "I think I can guess. I received a similar letter from a friend at the convent. The army have realised the church is hiding people. It was only a matter of time before they paid Rachel's convent a visit. But the sister in charge there has an evacuation plan. The nuns will do everything they can to protect her. Frank is having a look at some ideas for a new sanctuary now."

Isobel shook her head. "A new sanctuary? Darcy, she's coming here. In her letter she said she was on her way to S'aven. Here! This is not a sanctuary. Not for her." She felt her eyes starting to well.

Darcy shared Isobel's troubled look. They were both conspirators in Frank's world, but neither took pleasure in it.

"She said she has a job here already, that the nuns have sorted it all out for her."

Finally, he sighed and sat down beside the small nativity scene crafted by the altar. "Things outside of S'aven are bad. What you two saw in Red Forest…" Darcy shook his head. "It's everywhere now. The disease, the hunger. Safe Haven didn't get its name for nothing." He gestured to the room. "This place is a sanctuary. Not the best, but by no means the worst."

Isobel sat beside him. "Frank has so many enemies. If they found out about Rachel… I can't even imagine what would happen to her. And if she comes here, if she's here now, Frank will find her and he won't let her go."

Darcy shifted uncomfortably. This was ground neither of them liked to cover. When Frank Morris had offered to buy one of the girls, Darcy was not in a position to refuse. They needed to move and he'd only found a place for one of them. Frank was the answer and he was so generous, he would see that both girls were comfortable, he would dedicate everything he had to the Reacher cause. All the people Frank would help—just for one girl. Darcy knew that the choice would save one while condemning the other.

Isobel knew that too and her father's words rolled around her head, becoming more instinct than memory. She had stepped forward, volunteered her life for her sister's. And if she had known what awaited her in Frank Morris' care she would still have made the same choice.

"I don't want her to do what I've had to do," Isobel confessed. "And I don't want her to know what I have done for her either."

"You have nothing to be ashamed of," Darcy started.

"I prostituted myself. I allowed men to have sex with me and I used my powers to steal their secrets. And do you know what Frank has done with those secrets? Every one of them has ended up with someone dead. I'm just fuelling Frank's paranoia. Back at the start, I thought I was helping him. But I'm not, I'm making him insane."

"You are not responsible for the man Frank is. I am the one who let him have you." Darcy paused, sparing a glance at his saviour.

It was Isobel's turn to comfort him. She squeezed his arthritic hands. "I never told you, but when we arrived in S'aven, I knew where to come. We found you so quickly. I think back to that time, how we made our way here. It all just fell into place, but it was only when I arrived that I knew where I was going."

"A lot of Reachers have said that to me," Darcy said.

"What if Rachel comes back here?"

"Then it will be His will."

"She's special, I've always felt that. You'd think I'd be jealous that Dad favoured her life over mine. He made me run, but he would carry her. He told me to look after her, not to keep us both safe. I should be outraged, but I just feel, deep in my heart, that she is special and I will do anything to keep her safe. We haven't spoken in ten years and I still would do anything for her."

"Then He will keep her safe. Whatever happens, whatever you need to do, remember that you are special too. And your sacrifice has not just saved your sister but saved countless others. How many Reachers live now, because of what you have given up for them? Trust in Him."

Frank coughed behind them. "We should go, our table is waiting."

She gave Darcy a hug. "Will you look for her?" she whispered.

"I never look for you, you only come to me if you need me."

"There's an envelope on your desk, Darcy. I'll bring the rest in the morning," Frank said.

"God bless you, Frank. Enjoy your dinner, and your celebrations."

9

A smiling woman arrived at the church. She stayed for two nights, her face always a mask when she was around the girls. The smile hid her unease. She was a smuggler and her luck was coming to an end. Taking Rachel would be her last successful run. Isobel watched from a distance as the woman led Rachel into a vehicle.

"Will she be safe?" Isobel asked Darcy as they drove away.

"She'll be in God's house, there isn't a safer place in the world."

"Will I ever see her again?"

"I'm sure you will."

She wouldn't. The car dissolved into the distance and the sisters were separated forever.

10

They were shown to their table in the restaurant. S'aven didn't have many eateries, but this was by far the best. Frank's mood had lightened. Isobel was sure now that he didn't know about her affection for Donnie. His face was animated as he recounted snippets from their tainted history. He poured them both wine while they waited for their starters.

"To the most successful partnership in S'aven," he said. "Ten years and still going strong."

"And many more to look forward to," Isobel added, keeping the bitterness from her voice.

She looked out across the street. A single car was parked there, engine running. She recognised the red-haired man in the driver's seat. *Donnie?* He looked terrified and she couldn't understand why.

Donnie stared at the couple in the restaurant. Minutes earlier he had fixed his bomb to the underside of their table. Why would Frank tell him to blow up his own table? He checked his phone. The text was clear enough. Frank's instructions blatant. Donnie realised too late.

The message wasn't from Frank. It was a set up. He leapt out of the car, running across the road. He grabbed the door handle to the restaurant just as the building exploded.

END

PREVIEW OF THE RUNNING GAME

Reacher Series #1

1

Five past eleven.

Rachel's shift should have finished three hours ago. She slammed her time card into the machine. Nothing. She gave it a kick, then another until it released, punching her card and signing her out for the night. The hospital locker room was unusually quiet. There was a nurse signing out for the night, two doctors signing in. Nobody spoke to each other—it wasn't that kind of place. Grabbing her threadbare coat from her locker, she drew it over her scrubs—the only barrier between her and the unforgiving October night. She walked through the ER waiting room, eyes fixed on the exit. You had to ignore the desperation. Three hours over a twelve hour shift, you had no choice but to pretend like you didn't care. Push past the mothers offering up their sick children like you could just lay your hands on them and everything would be better. Push past the factory workers bleeding out on the floor. Push that door open and get out. Get home. You had to. In six hours the whole thing would start again.

The first blast of cold air slapped the life into her aching body. The second blast nearly pushed her back inside. She tightened the coat around herself, but the icy wind still managed to weave its fingers through the thin material and loose seams. November was coming, and coming fast. She quickened her pace, trying to outrun the winter.

She hurried past the skeletal remains of another fallen bank, a relic of the days before the economy crashed and the country went to hell. Now the abandoned building housed those left to the streets: the too old, the too young, the weak, the stupid. Cops would be coming soon, moving them on, pushing them from one shadow to another until dawn or death, whichever came first. But for now they sat huddled around burning canisters, silently soaking in the heat as though they could carry that one flame through winter. They didn't notice Rachel. Even the most evil of men lurking in the doorways, waiting for helpless things to scurry past, overlooked the young doctor as she made her way home. Nobody ever saw her. At least they never used to.

Three – two – one.

Nine past eleven. Right on cue.

She felt someone watching her. It was always the same place, opposite the third window of the old bank. He was hidden, not in the bank but close. So close she could almost feel his breath on the back of her neck. She'd watched muggings before, these were desperate times and people took what they could when they could. There were rapes too, five this week, at least five that had needed medical care. It was a dangerous city and getting worse. But this was different. He— and for some reason she knew it was a he—did nothing. For a week he had been there, never betraying his exact position or his intentions, but she could feel him and the longer he waited the more he tormented her. He knew where she lived, where she worked, the route she took to the exchange store. And he escorted her home each night without ever showing himself. It made no sense. And that made it so much worse.

She wasn't intimidated easily; doctors in St Mary's couldn't be. It didn't matter that she was only five feet tall and looked like a strong wind would knock her down; she could still take care of herself. But the stalking had spooked her. The sleepless nights followed as she wondered who he was, what he wanted, if he knew.

There was nowhere for her to go in the city, no place she could hide, no escape. If she wanted to eat she had to work, and he would be waiting for her outside the hospital—watching, doing nothing. She was tired of it, tired of everything, but there was something she could do. She could make it stop, one way or another. Whatever he had planned, whatever he wanted to do to her, he would have to look her in the eye as he did it, because she was done running.

She stopped walking and turned.

The street was empty. But she could still feel him there. The buildings pressed their darkness into the street and the spattering of hissing lamplights did little to expose the nocturnal danger below. There was noise. There was always noise; voices, vehicles, the persistent buzzing of the electricity struggling to reach the edges of the city. So much going on, yet so little to see—a perfect place to hide.

"Okay you pervert," she whispered to herself. "Where're you hiding?"

The road stretched back into a tightrope. Gingerly, her feet edged back towards the ruined bank. She scanned the buildings around her, the upper windows, the ground level doorways, waiting for him to pounce. One step, two steps. Look. Nothing. She retraced her steps to the next building. Then the next. He felt so close—why couldn't she see him?

"You want me, well here I am, you freak. Come and get me!"

There was a shout from the bank. Someone running. A man. Her stomach clenched. She braced herself. He pushed by her, hurrying away. It wasn't *him*.

She turned, her eyes trying to make sense of what she was seeing. Then warm breath touched the back of her neck.

"Get down!"

The world went white.

With her face pressed into the filthy, cold road, Rachel waited. The ground beneath her trembled, but that was it. She frowned, waiting for something, trying to understand what she was doing lying in a stinking puddle at the side of the road. Hands were lifting her to her feet. She turned to the bank, but it was gone. Flames licked at the pile of rubble in its place. People stumbled from the wrecked building, choking and coughing, others with their eyes as wide as their mouths. But there was no sound, just staggered movement and growing heat. Rachel watched, feeling more curious than afraid. The silent panic was fascinating. She made to move and her ears exploded with noise. The shock of it knocked her back. Screaming, cries for help, the ringing of sirens came from every direction.

The ground shook again and the building exploded another mortar firework into the street. She felt her body being tugged away. But people were coming to help. People were still alive. She was a doctor, she was needed.

"I can help these people," she shouted trying to fight off the man holding her back.

"It's a lure bomb." The voice was so cool it made her freeze. She looked at the stranger and swallowed the clumps of gravel lodged in the back of her throat. She had wanted to meet him face to face but not like this.

He stared at her with blank eyes. The dead and dying meant nothing to him. He was there for her and her alone. His hand still held her shoulder, holding her back. The hand that had pulled her to safety. So many questions ran through her head but she could only push one out.

"A lure bomb?"

A small explosion that drew in the police, she raced to remember. *Followed by the bigger bomb that would blow them to pieces.* She turned back to the space where the bank should have been. More people were rushing to help, pulling at the arms and legs of the buried. If they were lucky bodies would come with them.

"We have to warn…" The man had gone.

The sirens grew louder.

Rachel drew in a steadying breath. *Three hours over a twelve hour shift – you have no choice but to pretend like you don't care.*

She started to run.

2

Charlie jolted awake in his chair, his face sodden with sweat. He wiped his forehead with his sleeve. Pain coursed up his back, reminding him of his nightmare. The recurring dream of the day it all went wrong. He fumbled through his pockets until he found his pills. The placebo was instantaneous, and the pain relief followed shortly after. He rubbed his eyes and returned to the camera positioned towards the apartment in the opposite tower block.

The lights were on, curtains open. Someone had come home and he'd missed it. His one job and he'd screwed it up. He kicked out at the crutch resting against his chair and watched as it skidded across the floor out of his reach. Flexing his hands he willed the crutch back to him. Nothing happened.

"Shit."

He lifted himself from his chair too quickly and his right leg buckled, knocking over the camera – only the most expensive bit of kit they owned. The lens cracked.

"Shit, shit, shit." He shouted from the floor. The shockwaves of pain started to subside. Anger and shame fought their usual battle, while the voice inside his head urged him to just quit already. And, as usual, a persistent nagging from his bladder brought everything into perspective. He carried a lot of indignity on his shoulders, the last thing he needed was to be found sitting in a pool of his own piss.

This wasn't how his life was supposed to be. Charlie Smith had been a legend. He was a Reacher, born with incredible powers and an arrogance that made anything possible. With his former self firmly in his mind, he rested his head on the floor and focused on the crutch again. His fingers stretched out, reaching for the plastic handle in his head. He could still sense the weight and feel of it with his powers, but to move it took an effort his brain struggled with. This should have been easy but his telekinetic powers were failing him. The camera shook, turned on its side and then stopped altogether. The effort was exhausting and embarrassing.

Slowly, because nowadays everything had to be done slowly, he edged himself over to his crutch and, with it in hand, he managed to make it to the bathroom. It was a small victory, but it was nearly enough to cheer him up. That was until he caught sight of himself in the broken mirror fixed above the sink. He used to have charisma. He used to be able to smile his way out of trouble. Now he was lucky if people didn't cross the street to avoid him. Greying hair, dull red eyes, pallid skin. He was thirty-three; he looked fifty; he felt like a pensioner. The great Reacher Charlie Smith—reduced to this. Things had changed so radically in just a year. One year, two months, and eight days.

The lock in the front door turned. Charlie straightened his clothes. Everything was normal, everything was fine. He could cope, of course he could cope. He checked his smile in the mirror and stepped out of the bathroom as his brother kicked open the door and then kicked it closed again, to make his point.

"Everything okay?" Charlie asked.

His younger brother wore a scowl so deep it could have been chiselled into his skull. Everything was clearly not okay. But with John it was impossible to tell how far up the disaster scale the situation was. Charlie had seen that same scowl when a job went sour and he'd seen it when someone spilt coffee on John's suit.

"What happened?"

John glanced away. He was annoyed with himself – never a good sign. Charlie braved a crutch-supported step towards him. There was a four year age gap between the two of them, and it had never been more apparent.

Charlie gestured for them to sit down at the fold-up table in the dining space. Most of the time John had everything under control. It was rare for him to make mistakes or miscalculations, and when he did he would beat himself up over it for days. He would need Charlie, a professional in screwing things up, to put everything into perspective.

"She saw me," John confessed.

"She saw you!" Charlie said in disbelief. "You're like a creature of the night, how the hell could see you? Jesus, most of the time I don't even see you and I know you're coming."

John's fists clenched and unclenched. He stood up to work off the tension and started to pace; short, quick steps, squeaking his leather shoes against the linoleum floor.

"There was an explosion. Some bastard left a lure bomb right on her route. I had to pull her away before the goddamn building fell on her."

Charlie pinched the bridge of his nose. Even when his brother messed up he still managed to do something right. "What you mean is you saved her?"

John glared at him. "You're missing the point."

Charlie rolled his eyes. Only John would get himself so worked up over saving the life of their mark. "Listen, do you think he'd pay us if he found out we let her die?" Charlie said.

"You don't know that. We have no idea what he wants her for!"

It was true, they didn't and the fact was starting to chafe. The infamous Smith Brothers always knew the cards on the table before the deck was even dealt. Charlie planned jobs like he was writing a script. Nobody ever missed a cue. At least that was how it used to be a year ago. A year, two months, and eight days. Since then the jobs had dried up. They were lucky to get the Rachel Aaron case and that was only because Charlie's old mentor put in a good word for them. But luck and even the backing of an old priest didn't make the unknown any less troubling. They were out of their depth and they were still only in the shallows.

"Maybe he wants her dead," John stated.

"If he wanted her dead he would have asked us to kill her," Charlie replied. "And if he wanted her dead he wouldn't be approaching a priest to see if he knew anyone who could find her. He wants her found John, that's all."

"I don't like it," John snapped. "This whole job feels off."

"I know." Charlie took a deep breath, his next sentence shouldn't have made him nervous but it did. "Which is why I'm going to do a little field work myself."

John never looked surprised, or happy, or anything other than mildly impatient, but when something pleased him his right eyebrow would lift ever so slightly. As it rose, Charlie felt a pang of guilt that he hadn't said it sooner.

"I thought you were a liability," John jibed.

"It's surveillance in a hospital John, who's going to blend in better, me or you?"

The eyebrow perched higher on John's forehead. He'd been patient with Charlie, more patient than Charlie felt he'd deserved, waiting for his brother to get back in the game instead of going out on his own. John hadn't lost his edge. He didn't have a problem with stairs. He could drink what he wanted. Sleep when he needed. There was nothing wrong with his abilities. Charlie was holding them both back, but he knew John still clung to the hope that one day Charlie would recover and things would go back to normal. And Charlie needed him too much to tell him that was never going to happen.

"You sure about this?" John asked.

"We need the money."

"What if he does want to kill her, or worse?"

Despite what Charlie had said it was always a possibility. They weren't working for the good guys on this one and the girl had been hard to find, even with Charlie's powers. It was not going to end well for her and maybe that was why Charlie hadn't asked enough questions.

"We need the money," Charlie assured him. "That has to be our priority." That wasn't him talking. Sure he'd done questionable things, bad things even, but he had morality and right now it was screaming inside his head that this was all wrong.

John nodded, and Charlie was relieved to see that John was sharing his sentiments. "Fine, but if it has to be done I'll do it."

"No, you don't need this on your conscience. I'll do it."

John gave him a look. "Are we seriously going to argue about who gets to kill her?"

"Has to," Charlie corrected. "When you say 'gets to kill her' you kind of make it sound like a bonus prize. And no, we're not going to argue because I'll do it." He didn't have to say because it was his fault all of this had happened – that was a given.

John folded his arms. "Okay, but I get to dispose of the body."

Charlie scowled. "Did you mean to say 'get to'?"

His brother smirked. He had a unique sense of humour.

3

It took eight years for the British Empire to fall.

Like dominoes, major players in Europe and the western world started to topple, one by one. Each country falling hard enough to ensure the chain reaction was cataclysmic across the globe. Historians disagree where the trouble started; some argue it went as far back as the Second World War when the powers in charge set to picking up the broken pieces of the world and gluing them back together. Others are more cynical, claiming that man was destined towards devastation as soon as the first communities were formed by primitive apes.

However it happened, the cracks had been under the surface for a long, long time, growing weaker and more unstable. Internal conflict kept many countries in a stalemate. Where poverty and war still had a stronghold the effect of what was about to happen would barely touch the Richter scale. But in places like America, France, and Britain, places that had settled comfortably into peace and grown rich from their warring neighbours, the disturbance would be off the charts.

It was the financial crisis that struck the first blow. Each country struggled to balance its homeland cashbook, taking more credit and lending out money until the value of currency plummeted. When the system fell apart civilised government started to crumble, unable to compromise political greed and public integrity. The people revolted, seeing big cats in the big cities squandering money while their families starved in the suburbs. In France and Britain the rioting lasted five years, erupting into a burst of devastating civil war. Places like Red Forest and further north became impassable trenches of conflict that even the militia couldn't conquer.

The civil unrest was brought to a temporary halt when disease started to spread through Yorkshire and Lancashire. Birth deformities, viruses, and contamination concerns separated Britain into two halves and all who could fled south to escape the troubles. Northern Britain was abandoned and even Wales and Cornwall found themselves lost in isolated beacons out of London's reach. Disease spread, terrorism battled prejudice, and before anyone had realised it, aid packets were being flown over from Germany and the Australians were holding rock concerts for British kids in poverty. Most of the country slummed, counties broke off, and suddenly all that anyone seemed to care about was the thriving capital, where business men still wore Armani and sipped espressos. And that was the hardest pill to swallow; despite what was happening less than a hundred miles away, London was still thriving in a modern utopia.

People fled to the great city; their safe haven which grew like a tourniquet around London. Looking to fill the rumoured jobs and sample the last remnants of the good life, most found, when they got there, that London was walled off with wire fences as tall as the buildings they were enclosing. The cops kept watch and if you couldn't pay, you weren't coming in. The gathering crowd clustered and culminated, and eventually Safe Haven, or S'aven as the locals called it, became a city in its own right; a city with rulers as powerful as any of the fat men sitting in parliament square, and just as ruthless.

Pinky Morris had been one of those men, or at least his late brother Frank was. Pinky was more of the Deputy Prime Minster, to cover the summer holidays. They arrived in S'aven, when it was still a town of tents and ramshackle buildings, to sell hooch and marijuana to the refugees. People were starving but they could all afford a couple of joints. Business grew rapidly and one day Pinky blinked and the Morris brothers were at the top of the pecking order with an entire city underneath them. Frank was the boss, all smiles and threats, and Pinky was always there to back his little brother up with brawn and attitude. Together they could do anything. And they did.

That was more than a decade ago, before Pinky lost his empire, lost his respect, lost his brother. He was about to turn fifty-five, he'd lost most of his hair, his stomach was starting to sag, and he was back to running a small drug cartel in the back of his wife's club like he was just approaching twenty. His life had circled and he was pinning everything he had on it starting again.

The walls of his office were plastered with photograph after photograph; a memorial to the good old days. The little frozen moments captured a time Pinky could barely believe had happened. Hundreds of historical faces stared at him from his cramped office at the back of the bar, scrutinising the state he was in. And why wouldn't they, they were from a time when he was on top and meant something in S'aven. Those glossy faces that surrounded him in his youth were gone now, mostly dead or hovering in the vicinity as haggard and as old and as spent as he was. What did they think of him now? It was a question he'd try to avoid asking himself. The answers only ever made him angry. After all it wasn't his fault he was fighting for space at the bottom of the sewers again; he was just a victim of circumstance.

But all of that was about to change. He could feel a ball vibrating in the pit of his stomach. It was ambition and it had been a long time since he'd allowed himself to dream. The depression was almost over.

His eyes fell on the face that occupied every single picture: his brother, Frank. Pinky had tried to change things when he died. He had to. Frank had left them penniless with a reputation as worthless as their bank balance. Pinky had watched Frank's demise, and he had decided to do things differently. He didn't want to rule the city in fear, watching his back in every reflection. He let things slide now and again. He let the Russians move closer to his territory. He went easy on his boys. And he watched as it all came apart. Frank would never have let it happen, Pinky could see that now. His brother wasn't perfect, but he was right for the city. S'aven needed a man like Frank Morris, and Pinky just regretted it had taken him seven sorry years to realise those shoes needed filling, not replacing.

The man sitting opposite him coughed, clearing his throat rather than trying to attract Pinky's attention. He used to be called Donnie Boom and his face was scattered across the wall beside nearly every picture of Frank, not that anyone would recognise him. Most of Donnie's face was melted away, scarred from the explosion seven years ago. Even Pinky had to second guess himself when Donnie first made contact again.

That was four months ago, and Donnie's grey eyeball still made Pinky's stomach churn. But even before the scars, Donnie was enough to give a grown man nightmares. Now he just looked like the monster he had always been inside. And after all this time apart Pinky had forgotten just how crazy his late brother's best friend actually was.

"You blew it up," Pinky stated with impatience. He rapped his fingers against the desk. His nails were bitten to the pinks of his fingers, the skin on his knuckles cracked and sore. They were the hands of an old man.

"I did what needed to be done."

"Under whose authority?"

Donnie eyed Pinky with intense frustration, that grey eyeball pulsating in its scorched socket. "Your brother's. That bitch killed him, she needed to be taught a lesson."

Pinky lifted his thick rimmed glasses and rubbed the tiredness from his eyes. Donnie didn't understand the situation in S'aven anymore, or he just didn't care. Blowing up the most reputable brothel in S'aven was like starting an underground war and he didn't have the man power or the money to fight it. He was beginning to regret allowing Donnie back into the fold despite all that Donnie was promising him.

"You need to lie low for a while."

"I can help with—"

Pinky raised his hand sharply. "You want to fucking help, you keep your bombs out of my city!" Pinky yelled, surprising himself.

He sat back in his chair and stared at Donnie. His temper was starting to get the better of him these days. He couldn't remember Frank ever yelling. He never had to; Frank commanded respect without it.

Pinky calmed himself and lowered his voice. "Enough buildings are going up around this place without you helping. People are going to be asking about you now, Donnie. My people are going to be asking about you."

"Then let them know I'm back. I don't get all this cloak and dagger shit."

"You don't get it. You put a bomb under my brother's table and blew him half way across S'aven!"

"I didn't mean to kill them. I told you, the instructions were from Frank's phone. I was set up."

"Exactly and you want the people who set you up on to us, do you? Whoever it was I want them with their guard down, do you understand me? You stay off the grid and don't come around here anymore. I'll call you when I need you."

"What about when you get the girl?"

"I'll call you. Once we have her, we have everything. But we have to play this carefully, Donnie. Frank pissed off a lot of people. We can't just assume it was Lulu Roxton that killed him. When we have the girl, we'll know."

Donnie nodded. He was crazy but he wasn't stupid.

"I appreciate what you're doing," he said running what was left of his hand through his matted red hair. "You didn't have to believe me."

"You took a risk coming back here, I figured you were either suicidal or telling the truth," Pinky told him.

"I had to," Donnie assured him. "I have to know who did it, Pinky. I loved Frank. What they made me do to him..." Donnie shook his head, close to crying – it was an unsettling sight. "You're right, I shouldn't be here. Sometimes it's hard for me to think. My head gets kind of messed up, from the explosion. I'll get out of your way."

He reached the door before he turned around. "You remember you said I'd get to finish them?"

Pinky nodded; he did remember. With that, Donnie left. There was no way Pinky was going to let some deranged, half mad pyromaniac finish anything.

"What did he want?" Pinky's wife stood in the open doorway.

"Revenge," Pinky replied.

Riva swayed into the room. For a woman in her forties she was still turning heads. She smiled at Pinky, it was a natural smile, unblemished by silicone and cosmetics like the rest of the wives he knew. Sometimes Pinky would look at her and wonder what the hell she was still doing with him. He wondered if she asked herself the same question.

"Any news on the girl?"

"They think they have her."

"Do you want me to send someone to get her?" The question set Pinky on edge. He still had men, not as many as the old days, but there was still an entourage. Only now his wife had her own money from the club and she was investing it all in a legal security firm which was making his own boys look like school kids. Using them would be better, but they were Riva's boys, Riva's bodyguards, Riva's heavies, Riva's assassins. Not his. He didn't like it.

Pinky shook his head. "I'm going to send a couple of the old guys." He didn't say 'my' guys for her benefit.

"What about those brothers?"

"We'll deal with them when she's safely locked away. This time it's going to be different, Riva. I'm going to get my city back."

Dear reader,

We hope you enjoyed reading *Safe Haven*. Please take a moment to leave a review, even if it's a short one. Your opinion is important to us.

Discover more books by L.E. Fitzpatrick at
https://www.nextchapter.pub/authors/le-fitzpatrick-science-fiction-author

Want to know when one of our books is free or discounted for Kindle? Join the newsletter at
http://eepurl.com/bqqB3H

Best regards,

L.E. Fitzpatrick and the Next Chapter Team

ABOUT THE AUTHOR

L E Fitzpatrick is a writer of dark adventure stories and thrillers. Under the watchful eye of her beloved rescue Staffordshire bull terrier, she leaps from trains and climbs down buildings, all from the front room of a tiny cottage in the middle of the Welsh countryside.

Inspired by cult film and TV, L E Fitzpatrick's fiction is a collection of twisted worlds and realities, broken characters, and high action. She enjoys pushing the boundaries of her imagination and creating hugely entertaining stories.

www.lefitzpatrick.com